ashes g...

The blade seemed to wink wink w...
harder and faster
HARDER AND FASTER.
ARDER AND FASTER. ...es got harder and fast...
wink wink wink
harder and faster
...arder and faster
e blade HARDER AND FASTER. ...
...faster
...d to wink wink wink
FASTER
...ot harder and faster ...he flashes got harder a...
...and faster The blade seemed to wink wi...
harder...The flashes got harder and
AND FASTER. harder and faster
HARDER... HARDER AND FASTE...
...ink wink wink
The blade seemed... ...ink win...
...er and faster The blade seemed...
The flashes ...arder ...shes go...
...eemed to wink wink wink
harder and faster harder
...ASTER...
...hes got harder and faster "HARDER...
...ade s... ...nk win...
...arder...

ade seemed to wink WiNk WiNk

Flashes got harder and faster

The Flashes got harder and

harder and faster

harder and faster

The blade seemed to wink WINK

HARDER AND FASTER

HARDER AND FASTER.

got harder and fa

to wink Wink wink

harder and faster

harder and faster

HARDER AND FASTER.

the blade seemed to wink

nd faster

ned to wink WiNk WiNk

got harder and faster

ND FAST

the Flashes got harder

er and faster

The blade seemed to wink

harder and faster

R AND FASTER.

The Flashes got harder a

HARDER AND FAST

harder and faste

wink Wink wink

HARDER AND FAST

The blade seemed to wink wi

The blade seemed

The blade seen

der and faster

the Flashes

the Flashes

seemed to wink WINK WiNk

harder and fast

harde

ashes got harder and faster

HARDE

HARDER AND FASTER

blade seemed to wink Wink wi

harder and faster

JON
FOR SHORT

JON
FOR SHORT

MALORIE BLACKMAN

with illustrations by
Vladimir Stankovic

www.malorieblackman.co.uk

LONDON BOROUGH OF WANDSWORTH	
9030 00003 3551 1	
Askews & Holts	25-Apr-2013
JF TEENAGE 11-14	£6.99
	WWX0010837/0020

First published in 2013 in Great Britain by
Barrington Stoke Ltd
18 Walker Street, Edinburgh, EH3 7LP

This story was first published in a different form in *Incredibly Creepy Stories* (Random House Children's Books, 1996) and was later published as 'Joe's Nightmare' in *The Stuff of Nightmares* (Random House Children's Books, 2007)

www.barringtonstoke.co.uk

ISBN: 978-1-78112-195-5

Printed in China by Leo

For Neil and Lizzy, with love

1

Soft footsteps sounded in the dark bedroom. The dim light of a torch danced across the walls. The footsteps slowed as they came closer to the bed. With great care and without a sound, the torch was placed on the bed-side table. A bright flash of metal glinted in the torch beam. The glare of a knife-blade ... And as the blade flashed down in the dim light, it seemed to wink, wink, wink ...

2

A woman spoke.

"Of course not!" she said. "To tell the truth, I feel kind of sorry for him. It would be better for him if he had died ..."

At first I thought I was still in a dream. Then I became aware that the voice was outside my head for once – not inside. So I had to be awake.

I turned my head to where the voice was coming from and opened my eyes. A nurse jumped back and stared at me. She must have thought I was fast asleep. She was really old – over 50 at least – with grey hair. The hair was tugged back into a pony-tail that was so tight it pulled her eyelids out towards her ears.

"I just came in to make sure you were all right," she said. Her voice was steady, but her lips were a thin slash across her face. "Can I get you anything?" she asked.

I shook my head. She left the room without another look at me. I closed my heavy eyes and in an instant I was asleep again. The bad dream came at once and washed me away like a tidal wave.

Soft footsteps sounded in the dark bedroom. The dim light of a torch danced across the walls. The footsteps slowed as they came closer to the bed. With great care and without a sound, the torch was placed on the bed-side table. A bright flash of metal glinted in the torch beam. The glare of a knife blade ... And as the blade flashed down in the dim light, it seemed to wink, wink, wink ... Arms came up to ward off the flashes of light, but it did no good. The flashes just got harder and faster. Harder and Faster ... HARDER AND FASTER ...

3

When I woke up this morning, my left arm had been taken. I knew it was no longer there because it hurt so much. My left side roared with pain. I'd only felt pain like it once before – when they took my right arm. That was ... just under a day ago? Or just over? Or a week ago?

In this place, I've lost all track of time. But this place is all I have now.

Because I can't remember.

What's wrong with me? Why did they take both my arms? I don't know. My mind is like an empty box.

I want to remember. I so want to remember. I get the feeling the doctors don't buy it when I say that, but it's the truth. I try to make myself remember what happened, why I ended up here, but every time the memory dances away from me like a shadow in a dark room. Every day I wake up and the memories are almost there. But when my mind reaches out for them, they slip away. I can no more hold on to them than I could hold water in a sieve.

My name is Jonathan. Jon for short. I'm ... 14, almost 15. It's hard work remembering even those many facts and the effort wears me out. I turn my head from left to right to look around. I'm in a hospital. I've been in hospital for a long time, only I can't remember why ...

Also, I don't remember this room. Have I been moved? I think so. But from where?

It is a small room with light-coloured walls. There is a door to my left and apart from that there is nothing in the room except the bed I lie on – at least, I think it's a bed. The only light comes from a small pane of frosted glass in the door.

4

The door to my room slid open. I waited a few moments before I turned my head. In spite of the pain, I had to be careful. I couldn't show anyone just how scared I was. Or how lonely.

I looked at the male nurse who stood in the door. His eyes were stone cold, stone hard. He didn't like me. That was very clear. But why not?

"I'm Nurse Barrett," the nurse said, and looked away.

I wanted to ask about my arms but my voice refused to work. And the nurse still refused to look at me.

"I've come to give you your drugs," Nurse Barrett said. "I'm going to roll you over onto your side so that I can give you a shot in your bottom. Doctor Black will be here to see you soon. She's a psychiatrist."

Then he said, "Just a moment," and went out of the room. Moments later he came back with the old lady nurse who had checked on me in the night.

"Joe Forman, number J42935," the old lady nurse said.

"Joe Forman, J42935," Nurse Barrett repeated.

I shook my head. That wasn't right. My name was Jon, not Joe. They had the wrong name.

The old lady nurse scooted out of the room without another word. Nurse Barrett rolled me over and jabbed me in my bum. It should have hurt, but it didn't. I couldn't feel a thing.

Nurse Barrett turned me onto my back. I smiled at him. I wanted him to like me so much – him and the other nurses. It was hellish to be so alone.

"Keep smiling," Nurse Barrett said as he stood up. "It won't do you any good. You won't pull the wool over Doctor Black's eyes. And I'll tell you something else ..."

He didn't finish his sentence because just then a voice said:

"Thank you, Nurse Barrett. That will be all."

"Oh, Doctor Black," Nurse Barrett said. "I was … I was just …" His voice trailed off.

I gave up trying to smile. It didn't feel right. Nurse Barrett left the room. Doctor Black slid the door shut and walked over to me. My head began to feel warm and fuzzy, like it was stuffed full of cotton wool. And heavy. So very heavy.

"That's it, Joe," said Doctor Black. "You go to sleep. It's the best thing for you." Her voice seemed to come from long ago and far away.

It's Jon, not Joe. I wanted to tell her that, but I couldn't open my mouth. I tried to fight against my heavy eyes. I must not fall asleep – that was when the bad dreams came ... But it was no good! My eyes shut by themselves. Moments later, I was washed away again.

Soft footsteps sounded in the dark bedroom. The dim light of a torch danced across the walls. The footsteps slowed as they came closer to the bed. With great care and without *a sound, the torch was placed on the bed-side*

table. A bright flash of metal glinted in the

beam of the torch. The glare of a knife-blade ...

And as the blade flashed down in the dim light,

it seemed to wink, wink, wink ... Arms came

up to ward off the flashes of light, but it did no

good. The flashes just got harder and faster.

Harder and Faster ... HARDER AND FASTER ...

His legs kicked off the bed covers, kicked up at

the glints and the winks. The flashes of light

moved up and down, up and down – hitting

at his arms, his legs. His legs twisted and

kicked ...

5

I opened my heavy eyes. The room was dim with evening light. And then the pain started. My knees were on fire.

I knew what that meant. They'd taken more of me.

My legs below my knees were gone. I bit down onto my bottom lip till my mouth filled with blood. My whole body shook with pain and fear. My lips were clamped shut but still sounds like whimpers burst out between them.

There was nothing I could do to stop them. Hot tears burned my eyes. If only the pain would stop. If only ...

The door to my room slid open and Doctor Black came in.

"Good! You're awake," she smiled. Then she saw the tears on my face.

"D-Doctor Black, please give me back my legs," I begged. "I didn't say anything when you took my arms but it was too much to cut off my legs as well. I didn't deserve that."

A deep frown came across Doctor Black's face. "There's nothing wrong with your arms or your legs. Look for yourself. You still have them all. We haven't done anything to them."

"PLEASE! I want them back!" I shouted at her. "You all sneak around me and whisper about me. You want to drive me crazy. But I won't let you do it. Do you hear? You're the ones who are crazy. You just wait till my mum comes to see me. You just wait ..."

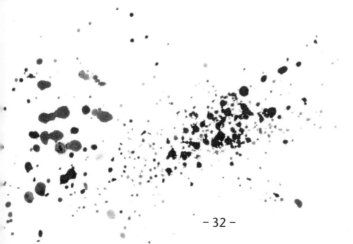

"Joe ..." she said.

The old lady nurse ran into the room.

"Get me the pain-killers on the top shelf of the drugs cupboard, Nurse Hill," Doctor Black ordered, then turned back to me. "Now then, Joseph ..." she began.

"Stop calling me that," I shouted. "My name is Jonathan. JONATHAN. I know what you're doing. You drug me till I don't know what's going on and then you cut bits off me, one by one ..." Tears streamed from my eyes. Gunk ran from my nose. And I couldn't wipe any of it away. The pain in my knees was not so bad now, but what did that matter? I'd lost more of myself. I didn't let them see when I cried for my arms. But to take my legs as well ...

Doctor Black walked over to me and threw back the bed covers.

"Look!" she said. "There are your arms, your legs ..."

I looked down, in spite of the fact that I knew it was a lie. My legs below my knees and both of my arms were gone. Just as I knew they would be.

The nurse came back with a small tray. Doctor Black picked up a needle from the tray, filled it from a little bottle and jabbed it into the top of my leg. Within seconds, my head was fuzzy again. Doctor Black handed the needle back to the nurse, who left the room at once. Doctor Black laid a cool hand on the top of one of my legs.

"Joe, can't you feel that?" she asked. The frown on her face was so deep that the lines around her mouth ran all the way down to her chin.

"The top parts are still there," I sniffed, fed up with this game the doctor was playing. "It's the rest I'm talking about. Below my knees."

I swallowed hard. "Come on, Jonathan, control yourself," I said to myself. "Don't let them drive you crazy. Don't let them ..."

That was when the pain-killer took over.

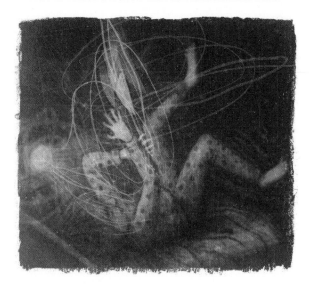

Soft footsteps sounded in the dark bedroom. The dim light of a torch danced across the walls. The footsteps slowed as they came closer to the bed. With great care and without a sound, the torch was placed on the bed-side *table. A bright flash of metal glinted in the*

beam of the torch. The glare of a knife-blade ...

And as the blade flashed down in the dim light,

it seemed to wink, wink, wink ... Arms came

up to ward off the flashes of light, but it did no

good. The flashes just got harder and faster.

Harder and Faster ... HARDER AND FASTER ...

His legs kicked off the bed covers, kicked up at

the glints and the winks. The flashes of light

moved up and down, up and down – hitting

at his arms, his legs. His legs twisted and

kicked ... He kicked out, kicked hard – but it

didn't do any good ...

6

When I opened my eyes again, Doctor Black was still there.

"Can I have some water, please?" I whispered.

The doctor picked up the plastic glass beside the bed, filled it and held it out to me. I just looked at her.

Doctor Black shook her head, but then she bent over me and placed the glass to my mouth. I was so thirsty I would have drunk all of the water but Doctor Black took it away before I was finished. I licked my lips. My tears slowed down. The pain in my knees was now just a dull throb.

Doctor Black pulled a tissue out of the box on my bed-side table and wiped my eyes and nose.

"Doctor Black, please don't let them take any more of me," I begged her. "Please ..."

She looked at me and shook her head again. I wondered what the odd look on her face meant. It was a mix of pity and something else that I found hard to make out.

There was a knock at the door.

"Joe, you have to go for an X-ray now. I'll see you when you get back," Doctor Black said.

"I'm not going anywhere," I said, and I turned my face away. But a porter I'd never seen before came in and lifted me and put me in a wheelchair. There was nothing I could do about it.

As the porter pushed the chair along the long hospital corridors, he spoke to me.

"Why did you do it?"

"Do what?" I asked, not sure what he meant.

"Do what?" he said. "Are you serious? You ... Y-You ..." He spluttered and choked as his words tripped over themselves in the effort to come out. Then it must have struck him how silly he sounded because he clamped his mouth shut.

I kept my own mouth shut too. I hadn't been trying to wind him up or make him angry. It was true that I had no idea what he was talking about. I couldn't remember.

As he pushed me along, I tried to fight to keep my eyes open. But I could still feel the pain-killer in my blood. As the wheel-chair rocked me, it took over. I failed ...

Soft footsteps sounded in the dark bedroom.
The dim light of a torch danced across the
walls. The footsteps slowed as they came
closer to the bed. With great care and without
a sound, the torch was placed on the bed-side

table. A bright flash of metal glinted in the beam of the torch. The glare of a knife-blade ... And as the blade flashed down in the dim light, it seemed to wink, wink, wink ... Arms came up to ward off the flashes of light, but it did no good. The flashes just got harder and faster. Harder and Faster ... HARDER AND FASTER ... His legs kicked off the bed covers, kicked up at the glints and the winks. The flashes of light moved up and down, up and down – hitting at his arms, his legs. His legs twisted and kicked ... He kicked out, kicked hard – but it didn't do any good ... And I saw his face for the first time ...

7

When I woke up, I was back in my bed – and the rest of my legs had been taken.

My whole body was numb. I lay very still and stared up at the ceiling until the old lady nurse walked into my room. I remembered her name was Nurse Hill. She had a dinner tray in her hand.

Nurse Hill didn't like me. But then, no one really liked me. It had always been that way. If only I could remember why ...

"I suppose there's no point in asking you to feed yourself," Nurse Hill said. Her lips curled down with dislike for me.

I didn't bother to answer. We both knew I had no way of feeding myself. My arms had been taken. Why did she have to be so cruel?

Nurse Hill sat down on the bed beside me.

"What is it?" I asked, and turned my head a little to look at the tray in her hands.

"Tomato soup and lamb chops," she said.

I didn't like meat but I was starving. And I had to eat. I had to get strong and well again. The sooner I was strong again, the sooner Mum could take me home. I'd be back with Mum and my brother, Joseph ...

I had a brother called Joseph!

At last, I'd remembered something else about myself. And that must be why they kept getting my name wrong. They had me mixed up with my brother!

I closed my eyes and tried to see my brother's face. But it wouldn't come to me. I had no memory of him. Was he older than me, or younger? Did I have any other brothers or sisters?

Lots of questions. No answers.

Nurse Hill took the plastic lid off the soup and the cover off the plate of lamb chops. She stood up and turned to me.

"You might have fooled some people with this act of yours, but you haven't fooled me," she hissed. "You can feed yourself or you can starve."

And with that she stormed out of the room.

I lay there and sniffed the lamb and soup smell.

But I had no legs to push myself up with. No

arms to feed myself with. I was so hungry

that the smell made me feel sick. I closed my

eyes and tried not to mind about the hunger

so much. I had to think of something else. To take my mind off my stomach I started to focus on my heart-beat instead. It was slower than before they took away my arms and legs.

What did I look like?

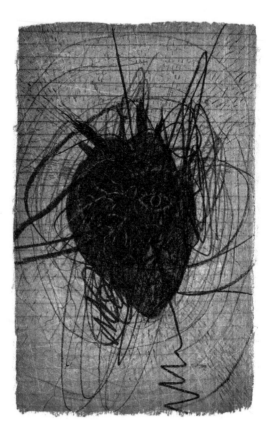

No ... I didn't want to see myself as I was now. I knew I wouldn't be able to bear it.

'Think of something else, Jon,' I told myself.

Even as I tried to listen to the slow beat of my heart, the rumble of my stomach got louder and louder. I made up my mind to go to sleep. To sleep for as long as I could. After all, what else was there for me to do? What else could they take away from me?

Maybe this time, the bad dream wouldn't come.

Soft footsteps sounded in the dark bedroom.
The dim light of a torch danced across the
walls. The footsteps slowed as they came
closer to the bed. With great care and without
a sound, the torch was placed on the bed-side
table. A bright flash of metal glinted in the

beam of the torch. The glare of a knife-blade ...
And as the blade flashed down in the dim light,
it seemed to wink, wink, wink ... Arms came
up to ward off the flashes of light, but it did no
good. The flashes just got harder and faster.
Harder and Faster ... HARDER AND FASTER ...
His legs kicked off the bed covers, kicked up at
the glints and the winks. The flashes of light
moved up and down, up and down – hitting
at his arms, his legs. His legs twisted and
kicked ... He kicked out, kicked hard – but it
didn't do any good ... And I saw his face for the
first time. Only it wasn't his face. It was my
face. My body – my face ...

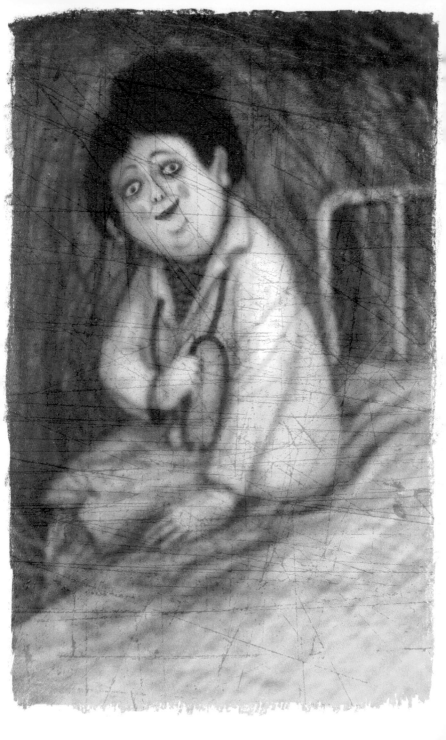

8

"Joe? Joe, can you hear me?"

I opened my eyes a crack. It was Doctor Black. She sat on the bed and smiled and asked me all kinds of questions. I gave her all the answers I could but all the time I was trying to drive the bad dream out of my head. It wouldn't go.

Doctor Black asked, "Joe, do you remember what happened two weeks ago? Do you remember the reason why you had to come to this hospital?"

I shook my head. "My name is Jonathan. Jon for short. And no, I don't remember. Why won't anyone tell me?"

"Do you really want to know?" the doctor asked, in a soft voice.

"Yes," I said. "I do. I want to know why everyone here hates me so much. I want to know why you've stolen my legs and my arms. I want to know ..."

There was a long time when no one spoke.

This was it. Now I would find out why I was here. I had to know. I needed to remember.

"I'm going to take a chance, here," Doctor Black said at last. "I think you should know what happened – what you did. I think you're ready. And it will help you."

And her voice was slow and careful as she told me, "Joe, you had a brother called Jonathan. He was your identical twin brother. You weren't close to each other. In fact, your Mum says that would be a very kind way to put it ..."

And she went on. I heard her words but they slid off me until there were too many to slide off and then they sunk into my flesh like razor-sharp spikes – and still she spoke. My body shook with horror and the more I shook, the more my body hurt.

And still Doctor Black went on. I wanted to yell, to howl and not stop. It was all lies. It had to be lies. I would never do that, could never do that – the horrific, mindless thing she spoke of. I wouldn't do that to anyone, let alone my own twin brother …

"No …" I whispered. "No, it's not true."

I had to do something to drown out her words. My sides started to hurt. My hips started to hurt.

I covered my ears with my hands and sat up, pulling my legs up to my chest.

"NO! NO! NO!" I hit out at the doctor with my fists. "Liar! Liar! Liar …"

All at once the room filled with people. I was pushed back onto the bed. I hit out at them all. Hit out at them with my fists and kicked at them with my feet till the room swallowed me up like a whirl-pool.

Doctor Black and the others faded into nothing.

Soft footsteps sounded in the dark bedroom.
The dim light of a torch danced across the
walls. The footsteps slowed as they came
closer to the bed. With great care and without
a sound, the torch was placed on the bed-side
table. A bright flash of metal glinted in the

beam of the torch. The glare of a knife-blade ...
And as the blade flashed down in the dim light,
it seemed to wink, wink, wink ... Arms came
up to ward off the flashes of light, but it did no
good. The flashes just got harder and faster.
Harder and Faster ... HARDER AND FASTER ...
His legs kicked off the bed covers, kicked up at
the glints and the winks. The flashes of light
moved up and down, up and down – hitting
at his arms, his legs. His legs twisted and
kicked ... He kicked out, kicked hard – but it
didn't do any good ... And I saw his face for the
first time. Only it wasn't his face. It was my
face. My body – my face ...

There is just me and my brother left in the whole, wide world.

Jon lies there and looks up at me. His eyes burn into mine. His blood soaks the bed sheets. It drips down from the knife in my hand.

Drip. Drip. Drip.

He whispered my name over and over before he died.

Joe ... Joe ... Joe ...

9

When I woke up this morning, they had taken my whole body.

There's nothing left of me now except my head and my brain, lying here in the middle of the pillow on this bed.

I don't know how they're keeping me alive – I don't care. I just wish someone would tell me what I did to deserve this. I really do want to know.

What did I do?

I wish ... How I wish I could remember.

All I know for sure is that my name is
Jonathan.

Jon for short.

And I'm 14, almost 15.

de seemed to wink WiNK WiNk

lashes got harder and f

harder and faster

HARDER AND FASTER.

o wink Wink wink

arder and faster

d faster

ed to wink WiNk WiNk

got harder and faster

r and faster

R AND FASTER.

wink Wink wiNk

der and faster

seemed to wink WiNK WiNK WiNK

shes got harder and faster

lade seemed to wink Wink wi

harder and faster

The Flashes got harder and f

harder and faster

The blade seemed to wink Wink w

HARDER AND FASTER

lashes got harder and fas

harder and faster

HARDER AND FASTER.

The flashes got harder

The blade seemed to wink w

The Flashes got harder ar

harder and faster

HARDER AND FAST

The blade seem

harder

HARDER

ade seemed to wink wink wink
The Flashes got harder and
flashes got harder and faster
harder and faster
harder and faster
The blade seemed to wink wink
HARDER AND FASTER.
the flashes got harder and fa
HARDER AND FASTER.
to wink wink wink
harder and faster
harder and faster
the blade seemed to wink
and faster
HARDER AND FASTER.
ned to wink wink wink
AND FAS
the flashes got harder
got harder and faster
got harder
er and faster
The blade seemed to wink
harder and faster
The Flashes got harder
R AND FASTER.
HARDER AND FA
harder and faste
wink wink wink
HARDER AND
HARDER AND FA
The blade seemed to wink w
The blade se
rder and faster
The flashes
the flashes
seemed to wink wink wink
harder and faster
hard
ASTER.
"HARDE
shes got harder and faster
blade seemed to wink wink w
harder and faster